First published in Great Britain in 1994
by Simon & Schuster Young Books
Campus 400
Maylands Avenue
Hemel Hempstead
Herts HP2 7EZ

Typeset in Garamond Light by Goodfellow & Egan Ltd, Cambridge
Printed and bound in Belgium by Proost International Book Productions

British Library Cataloguing in Publication Data available.

ISBN: 0 7500 1258 7
ISBN: 0 7500 1386 9 (pb)

The Little Apple Tree

Inga Moore

SIMON & SCHUSTER
YOUNG BOOKS

Lucy's father was a gardener.
He worked in a beautiful garden looking
after all the trees and flowers.
Lucy often went with him to the garden.
This was something she loved to do.

Round about the time Lucy was born
her father had planted a little apple tree.
Lucy couldn't walk as well as other little girls.
But, whenever she went to the garden,
she always walked right down the path –

round the fish pond,

over the wooden bridge,

through the gate,

down by the berry bushes . . .

to the corner by the cabbage patch where the little apple
tree stood.

Lucy loved the little apple tree. Perhaps this was because
it was small and frail like her. For though her father
looked after it in every way, it hadn't grown as
it should. Nor had it blossomed. Of course
this meant it never bore
any fruit.

Lucy's father shook his head.
"It will have to come out," he said.
"Oh no. NO!" cried Lucy. "Don't pull it out.
It will blossom. I *know* it will."
So Lucy's father gave the little apple tree another
chance, and left it where it was for one more year.

Spring came round again. Birds built their nests. The
sun shone. In the garden everything was growing.
The little apple tree stretched out its branches.
"Look," said Lucy, showing her father
the pink buds of blossoms which
grew at their tips.

Each day she walked down the path to see if the buds had opened, only to find them shut tight.

As the days went by, they drooped sadly.

Then, just as they had done every year, one by one, the buds of the little apple tree began to wither and fall.

Lucy's father went to fetch his rope and spade.

"Wait," cried Lucy.

But Lucy's father wouldn't wait. There was
no place in his garden for a useless tree.

"Couldn't we wait a *little* longer?"
she pleaded.

In the end he agreed to wait
for just one more day.

Then, that afternoon, as often
happens in springtime,
a sudden storm blew up.
Winds tossed the trees until
the ground was scattered
with their leaves and twigs.
Even branches tumbled down.
With one of them was a
thrushes' nest.
Lucy picked it up. Inside
there were six speckled eggs.
They were still quite warm . . .

and, all but one, unbroken.

The thrushes hovered beside
her, frantic with worry.

Lucy knew she must put the
nest back into a tree at once.

But the trees in the garden were all very tall.

With the thrushes fluttering behind her . . .

Lucy made her way

to the little apple tree.

In its strongest fork she
carefully balanced the nest.
The thrushes perched nervously
beside it, afraid that it would fall again.
But the little apple tree held it firmly, never
letting go its grip, no matter how hard the wind blew.

Next morning the storm had passed. The world woke
to a clear blue sky. Birdsong filled the air as Lucy hurried
down the path towards the little apple tree.
As she drew near, she heard the sweet song of a thrush.
And, looking up, she saw the cock-thrush on the garden
wall singing with all his might.

Below, in the branches
of the little apple tree,
sat his mate – safe
on her nest.

Lucy went to find her father.
"Come and see," she said.
But it wasn't the thrushes she wanted to show him –
or their nest . . .

From top to bottom the little
apple tree was covered in
pale pink blossom.

This time Lucy's father put away his rope and spade for good, and the little apple tree stayed where it was in the corner by the cabbage patch. Every day Lucy came to admire its blossom, and after the blossom had faded she searched for the first signs of fruit.

By now the thrushes' eggs had hatched.
Five hungry chicks kept the birds busy all day long.

In time the chicks turned into fledglings.
And when, at last, they left the nest,
Lucy watched as the little apple tree held them steady,
never swaying, spreading its leaves beneath them as
they hopped uncertainly from branch to branch.

Eventually the fledglings flew away. So did the thrush and his mate. But they never forgot the little apple tree.
Year after year they came back to build their nest in its branches.
The little apple tree blossomed and grew.
It didn't grow very big – and it never had many apples.
But the apples it had were the best apples Lucy's father had ever tasted.